For Ruth

Published by
PEACHTREE PUBLISHERS, LTD.
1700 Chattahoochee Avenue
Atlanta, Georgia 30318-2112

www.peachtree-online.com

Text and illustrations © 2001 by Ken Brown

First published in Great Britain in 2000 by Andersen Press

Printed and bound in Italy

10 9 8 7 6 5 4 3 2 1
First Edition

ISBN 1-56145-240-8

Cataloging-in-Publication Data is available from the Library of Congress

The Scarecrow's Hat

Written and Illustrated by
Ken Brown

PEACHTREE
ATLANTA

"That's a nice hat," said Chicken to Scarecrow.

"Yes, it is," replied Scarecrow. "But I'd rather have a walking stick. I've been standing here for years now, and my arms are so tired. I'd love a walking stick to lean on. I'd swap my hat for a walking stick any day."

Now Chicken didn't have a walking stick, but she knew someone who did.

"That's a nice walking stick," said Chicken to Badger.

"Yes, it is," replied Badger. "But I'd rather have a piece of ribbon. It gets hot and stuffy underground, so I prop my door open with my stick. But I'm always tripping over it. If I had a ribbon, I could *tie* the door open. I'd swap my walking stick for a ribbon any day."

Now Chicken didn't have a ribbon, but she knew someone who did.

"That's a nice ribbon," said Chicken to Crow.

"Yes, it is," said Crow. "But I'd rather have some wool. My nest is on this high, stone ledge, and it's very hard to sit on. I'd love some warm, soft wool to line it with. I'd swap this ribbon for some wool any day."

Now Chicken didn't have any wool,
but she knew someone who did.

"That's a nice wool coat," said Chicken to Sheep.

"Yes, it is," replied Sheep. "But I'd rather have a pair of glasses. I have to keep a lookout for the wolf, and my eyes are not as good as they used to be. I really need a pair of glasses. I'd swap some of my wool for a pair of glasses any day."

Now Chicken didn't have a pair of glasses, but she knew someone who did.

"That's a nice pair of glasses," said Chicken to Owl.

"Yes, it is," said Owl. "My old ones broke, so I had to get a new pair. But I'd rather have a blanket. The sun streams through my window and keeps me awake all day, which wouldn't matter if I had a good, thick blanket to sleep under. I'd swap my glasses for a blanket any day."

Now Chicken didn't have a blanket, but she knew someone who did.

"That's a nice blanket," said Chicken to Donkey.

"Yes, it is," replied Donkey. "But I'd rather have a few feathers. The flies drive me crazy, buzzing around my ears. My tail isn't quite long enough to flick them away. But if I had some long feathers tied to the end of it, I could swat them easily. I'd swap my blanket for a few long feathers any day."

Quick as a flash, Chicken pulled out one, two, three of her longest feathers and tied them to Donkey's tail.

Donkey was delighted and, true to his word, swapped his blanket for the feathers.

Chicken took the blanket to Owl—
who swapped it for his glasses (the old ones, of course).

She took the glasses to Sheep—
who swapped them for her wool.

She took the wool to Crow—
who swapped it for her ribbon.

She took the ribbon to Badger—
who swapped it for his walking stick.

Finally, she took the walking stick to Scarecrow. With a grateful sigh of relief, he leaned his tired old arms on the stick and gladly swapped it for his battered old hat.

Chicken took the hat and filled it with fresh, sweet-smelling straw….

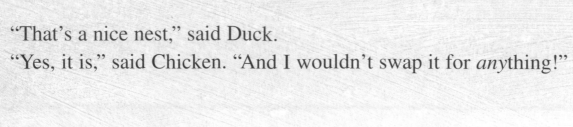

"That's a nice nest," said Duck.
"Yes, it is," said Chicken. "And I wouldn't swap it for *anything!*"